Danika's Totally Terrible Toss

Other books in the
Secret Keeper Girl Series

Yuzi's False Alarm

"T" is for Antonia

Just Call Me Kate

Danika's Totally Terrible Toss
The Legend of the Purple Flurp

Dannah Gresh
author of Secret Keeper Girl

Moody Publishers

CHICAGO

Scripture quotations marked *The Message* are from *The Message*, copyright © by Eugene H. Peterson 1993, 1994, 1995. Used by permission of NavPress Publishing Group.

Interior design: JuliaRyan | www.DesignByJulia.com
Cover and Illustrations: Andy Mylin
Some images: © 2008 JupiterImages Corporation

Library of Congress Cataloging-in-Publication Data

Gresh, Dannah.
  Danika's totally terrible toss : the legend of the Purple Flurp / Dannah Gresh ; [illustrations by Andy Mylin].
     p. cm. -- (Secret Keeper Girl series)
  Summary: After accidentally hitting Mrs. Hefty with her brown bag lunch, sixth-grader Danika, a popular overachiever, winds up in after-school detention, where she meets three other girls who join her in forming the "Secret Keeper Girl Club." Includes a mother/daughter Girl Gab assignment.
  ISBN 978-0-8024-8702-5
[1. Clubs--Fiction. 2. Middle schools--Fiction. 3. Schools--Fiction. 4. Popularity--Fiction. 5. Christian life--Fiction. 6. Friendship--Fiction.]
  I. Mylin, Andy, ill. II. Title.
  PZ7.G8633Dan 2008
  [Fic]--dc22

                        2008026481

We hope you like this book from Moody Publishers. We want to give you books that help you think and figure out what truth really looks like. If you liked this and want more information, you and/or your mom can go to www.moodypublishers.com or write to . . .

Moody Publishers
820 N. LaSalle Boulevard
Chicago, IL 60610

1 3 5 7 9 10 8 6 4 2

Printed in the United States of America

To my Lou Lou,
who helped me write this!

Danika's Totally Terrible Toss

CHAPTER 1

Danika's Purple Flurp

Tonight I'm going to win the Miss Teeny Pop Pageant.
There's no easy way to explain that absurd thought
except to say that I'm growing up in Marion, Ohio. It's
the Popcorn Capital of the World, and life revolves
around the annual Popcorn Festival.

"Good luck tonight, Teeny Pop!" mocked Chad Ferner,
slamming his locker shut. Ferner was once the awkward
boy I'd survived second grade square dancing with. He
wasn't so awkward anymore with his wavy chestnut hair
and deep blue eyes. We have never liked each other,
though, since those totally embarrassing do-si-dos.

"Here she is . . ." he sang, waving his arms dramatically
toward me to the tune of the Miss America theme song,
". . . she's Miss Teeny Pop!" Everyone in the hallway was
laughing, and I couldn't decide if they were laughing at
him or at me.

I glared really hard until I was sure that my dark-brown Asian eyes might possibly pop from their sockets. When Ferner didn't back off, neither did I. I leaned in to his face until I could smell the Nerds on his breath.

"Chillax, Da-neeka," Ferner said, mispronouncing my name on purpose. He always does that.

Then, as suddenly as he disrupted my day, he slipped silently away. I watched him walk down the hall and through the big red doors that led to the microcosmic world of the Rutherford B. Hayes Middle School cafeteria.

I opened my locker and carefully placed my *Advanced Pre-Algebra* textbook to the far left of the top shelf, right next to *Biology for the Young Scholar*. Arranging my books in alphabetical order seemed only natural to me, but Mom says it's odd even if my IQ rivals that of Einstein. I knew he was really messy based on those famous pictures of him and his wacky hair. I didn't want to end up like that, so I alphabetize my books . . . and my nail polish.

Adjusting my bright yellow headband, I checked my look in the pink marabou-trimmed mirror hanging on the door of my locker. For a moment, I dreamed of what my black-as-night hair would look like topped by the Teeny Pop crown.

It doesn't matter what Chad Ferner or anyone else thinks, I want to win that crown! I thought.

My mom entered me into my first Popcorn Festival pageant when I was six. That was the same year they found out just how smart I was, and Mom thought it would be good if she and Dad let me do something "frilly and superficial" to "balance me out." Those were the actual words my dad used. I remember.

So, that year I dressed up in a golden yellow dress for the modeling competition and then, like a can of Jolly Green Giant peas for the commercial presentation. I sang, "Peas, say you'll love me!" It doesn't get much more frilly or superficial than that! I got first prize in my age group, as I have every single year since then. This is the first year I'm old enough to win the big title, Miss Teeny Pop, and I want it so badly!

After all, this year's big prize is four front-row seats to the Alayna Rayne concert. She's a totally fab singer who sells out concerts in minutes. Even my dad, who's richer than Daddy Warbucks and would pay *anything*, hasn't been able to get tickets. He's tried five times. Alayna's coming to

Cleveland in two weeks and I really want those tickets.

When I had decided that every hair was in place, I grabbed my hot pink and lime green Vera Bradley lunch bag and a brown sack out of my locker. I slammed the door and headed for the cafeteria. The brown sack had an extra-special dessert. Inside was a container filled with Mom's legendary Purple Flurp. It's a legend because it's the only food to ever win the Popcorn Festival blue ribbon that *didn't* have popcorn as an ingredient. It's *that* good!

GO TO secretkeepergirl.com and type in the secret word 'Flurp' to get the recipe for Purple Flurp!

"Hey, Laney," I said sitting down next to the most popular girl in sixth grade, blonde-haired, blue-eyed, genetically perfect Laney Douglas. She was wearing all pink, which she says is her "signature color."

"Hey," said Laney and her stuck-like-glue sidekick Riley Peterson. They always say hello in unison. If I didn't like them, it would honestly make me toss my cookies.

When I first stepped into the jungle of middle school, I quickly learned the first lesson of survival: you're not defined by who you are, but by who is sitting next to you at lunchtime. That week, Rachel, Chondra, Kiley, Abigail, and Kelsey—the other regulars who are seated with us today—took a vote led by Laney and Riley. They decided I could sit with them.

Our conversations never go any deeper than the pink clothes on Laney's back and the topic of boys. In a crunch, we talk about the food on our table.

"So, like, what exactly is *in* powdered soup?" asked Laney. She watched me pour the energy-boosting powder my mom had packed for me into a Thermos of hot water.

"Hmmm?" I said. "I dunno."

"Potato starch." I began reading the packet out loud. "Salt. Dried minced onion. Powdered pork?"

"Whoa!" exclaimed Laney. "Bad ending for that pig!"

We laughed much louder and longer than we should have. Why? Because we knew everyone in sixth grade was watching our table. As I fake-laughed, I caught the gaze of Katie Harding walking toward us. Our moms are practically best friends. I guess we used to be, too.

Katie was wearing a really cool T-shirt with a red heart on it over a striped long-sleeve shirt. I thought it looked really great. Apparently, Laney didn't think so.

"I wonder where she shops . . . UglyRUs?" Laney said almost loud enough for Katie to hear.

"I think it's UglyR*Her*!" whispered Riley.

The whole table laughed again really hard.

Keep walking, Katie! I pleaded in my head. I put my left hand up to my forehead like a visor and looked down. *Keep walking!*

She took the clue and abruptly turned and walked to a table where she sat all by herself. She looked lonely.

I suddenly felt **sick**.

"Hey, Da-neeka," teased a guy's voice from behind me. I was going to ignore it, but when I felt someone flick my hair, I looked back. Ferner!

"Hey," I responded coolly. He moved on.

"He likes you," whispered Laney, leaning across the table and into me.

My eyes grew wide in fear.

"*You* like *him*," she accused.

"No way!" I said. Dad would kill me if I got boy crazy. I might as well start carving the tombstone.

"We just danced together . . ." I started to explain about square dancing in second grade and hating it, but Laney didn't let me finish.

"You danced together," she teased. "Hey girls! Danika and Ferner danced together!"

The laughter erupted even more loudly this time, drawing the attention of the world's most bizarre lunch lady, Mrs. Hefty. She lives up to her name quite easily. I'm not sure what body mass index really is, but I think Mrs. Hefty has it. The seams on her white uniform work really hard to hold everything in place.

"What's going on over here?" she asked as she waddled over to our table.

No one answered her.

"Was that joyful laughter?" she asked. She didn't stop for an answer, but started talking at a breakneck pace like she always does when she gives her infamous Cafeteria Life Lessons. "There is joyful laughter. Yes. That is laughing *with* people, and then there's another kind. That's when you laugh *at* people. We can't have any of that in my cafeteria. Can we? No, no, no. No we can't!"

She drew out that last word and when she cut it off with a sharp "t," she sprayed enough spittle from her wet lips to shine my dad's red sports car.

After a moment of staring at us to make her point, her cheeks burst into red bulbs as she smiled. Then she waddled off.

13

Laney quickly scrawled something on a scrap of paper and passed it to me. In curly handwriting it said . . .

"Mrs. Hefty is a big _____."

Just as I read it and imagined what the blank would say, I felt the chill of a shadow looming over me. Mrs. Hefty was back.

"Well, Ms. McAllister, let me see that note there!" She paused to read it. "Oh, troublesome! Why don't you finish that sentence for me?"

"But, I-I d-didn't write it," I stammered.

"I didn't ask if you wrote it," cooed Mrs. Hefty as she tried her best to be angry. She shook the note in her hand for effect. "I asked you to finish it."

"*But!*" I pleaded.

She just stared down at me.

"Ummm . . . well . . . Mrs. Hefty is a big . . ." I stalled for time drawing my answer out, then I suddenly blurted out a terrible, no-good word . . .

". . . meanie?" I said it more as a question.

Mrs. Hefty's smiling face dropped. Her big, rosy cheeks sagged into puffy wrinkles. *Uh, oh*, I thought.

"Ms. McAllister, your lunch period is over," she announced as happily as ever. "Let's go! You and I have an appointment with Principal Butter. Up you go. This way. Follow me."

Fine! I thought. *I'll go, but I'm taking my mom's Purple Flurp with me!*

I grabbed the little brown sack and marched off.

"Hold it!" I heard Mrs. Hefty say from behind me. "What's in *that* bag, Ms. McAllister?"

I turned to look at her. Her chubby finger was aimed right at my prized sack of **Purple Flurp**.

"Is that *food*?" she prodded. "Ms. McAllister, what does *that* sign say?" She used her finger to emphasize the big sign above the red doors. I looked up to read it: *Positively No Food Outside the Cafeteria!*

Suddenly, a surge of anger flashed through every inch of me, turning my normally dainty, girlish twelve-year-old self into a hulk of fury. I placed my precious brown bag into my right hand. I wound my arm up like I'd seen softball pitchers do and aimed for the garbage can two feet to the left of Mrs. Hefty. I threw the bag like a slow-pitch softball with a long rainbow arc.

My Purple Flurp never made it to the garbage can.

15

It managed to find its way out of the brown bag. As it spiraled through the air in what seemed like slow-mo, the lid of the container disconnected like the launching sequence of a space rocket. In that moment, its purple-gooey contents were unleashed into space.

Then my Purple Flurp-pitch nailed Mrs. Hefty in the left temple.

Apparently, I'll never be a softball player.

Danika's Totally Terrible Tiss

CHAPTER 2

Danika's Detention Disorder

As I stood in Principal Butter's office, a big blob of purple goo dripped from Mrs. Hefty's face. She'd already used her chubby little fingers to squeegee the Purple Flurp from her eyes, but the rest stayed right where it had landed as she told the sad tale of what had happened. Principal Butter looked at her in disbelief while the big clock on the wall seemed to tick its disapproval.

"Danika," asked a dazed Principal Butter, "what on earth were you thinking?"

I wanted to tell them both about the number one rule for survival in middle school: you're not defined by who you are, but by who you sit by at lunchtime.

I wanted to tell them how **lonely** Katie Harding looked at lunch.

I wanted to tell them that Laney Douglas embarrassed me when she accused me of liking Ferner.

I wanted to tell them that the other girls were laughing at me for dancing with him, but they didn't understand it was just second grade square dancing and we *hated* it.

Most important, I wanted to tell them that I was aiming for the garbage can, *not* Mrs. Hefty's left temple.

Instead, I just bit my lip to fight off tears.

"Well," said Principal Butter in a quiet voice, "we don't actually have a policy for . . ." He paused and cleared his throat. "Well, for . . . throwing a sack at lunch aides. Let me take a moment to think."

The clock ticked even more loudly.

Mrs. Hefty's face dropped another glob of Purple Flurp onto the floor.

Principal Butter sat down in his big wooden chair. He folded his hands together and just stared at a leaky spot in the ceiling for like five minutes.

"Danika," he finally said with an air of disappointment. "I'm afraid I have some bad news. First, I think I have no choice but to give you a three-day after-school detention."

He pulled a pad of pink slips from his drawer, scribbled on the top one, ripped it off, and handed it to me.

"You'll report Wednesday," he said.

I nodded softly and put my head down.

"Second," he said, "I'm sure you are aware that *Mrs.* Butter is the chairwoman of the Teeny Pop Pageant. This city has a long history of upstanding young women winning that pageant."

Upstanding? I thought. *What on earth does that mean?* I don't think Principal Butter is that old, but sometimes it seems like he might be a ninety-year-old man who's been locked in a box for the past sixty years. Most of his vocabulary is made up of words only dead people, like Abraham Lincoln, would have used.

"Danika," he said, "I'm afraid I'll have to report this unusual occurrence to my wife so she and the committee can make a decision about your participation."

My head jerked up. My long black hair shook loose from my headband.

"But . . ." I pleaded. "You can't . . . I . . ."

I couldn't hold the tears back anymore. Without even asking, I darted for the bathroom.

Changing classes was miserable for the rest of the afternoon. I was suddenly the most talked about girl in school, a fact that I was pretty sure Laney Douglas would not like one little bit. Everyone looked my way and whispered when I walked by. Usually they were smiling. Often they'd give me two thumbs-up. A few even gave me a shout out.

"Way to go, McAllister!" hooted Trevor Kenworth, the school's biggest loudmouth.

I felt like my head might explode. Was it actually possible that doing something *bad* was actually . . . well, uh . . . *good*?

When I got to my locker between sixth and seventh periods, I ran into Ferner talking to some new girl with a hairdo I can only describe as a mini-'fro.

". . . the Popcorn Capital," Ferner said to the new girl as he plopped his books into his locker. "Ask Miss Teeny Pop to tell you about it," he said in his mock-tone, slamming his locker shut. He tugged on my hair when he walked past me.

"Nice pitch, Teeny Pop!" he taunted.

Ugh!

"Walk with me, " I pleaded to the girl, closing my locker door. I wanted to get out of the hall as fast as I could and into my classroom. "OK. Basically, we live and breathe popcorn here. It all revolves around the Popcorn Festival, which is this weekend."

"Cool!" said the girl, whose beautiful chocolate skin seemed to shimmer.

"This weekend, the air in Marion will smell like fresh buttery popcorn," I said. "When I say we breathe it, I mean it!"

I told her everything I could squeeze in between my locker and my Honors Math classroom. "Since as long as I can remember, my mom has been entering the Popcorn Cooking Contest and winning." I began quickening my pace to get it all in. "Two years ago she took first place for her Purple Flurp."

"Purple Flurp? Isn't that the stuff the girl at lunch . . ."

I quickly interrupted her. "You should totally come out to the Festival this weekend!" I told her about Sky Pop, the fireworks finale that my dad always donated each year.

"He does fireworks all over the world," I said proudly.

I never even got to tell her about the Teeny Pop pageant, but we'd arrived at my class.

"Well, umm . . . what's your name?" I asked.

"You-zee." She pronounced her name carefully.

"Right," I said, wondering what kind of name that was. "Well, welcome to Rutherford B. Hayes."

"Thanks! Well, I guess I'll see you later," said Yuzi, and she walked off. I thought to myself that she was kind of cool.

"Yoo-hoo, Danika!" I heard Laney's voice calling. "Gotta go, Mom!" I looked back to see her snapping her cell phone closed, even though we're not allowed to use them in school.

She walked toward me with her messenger bag on one arm and my lunch bag in her other hand. Of course Riley was with her.

"You're not actually talking to that *African* girl," whispered Riley. Riley and Laney had a bad habit of saying even the most factual things in the meanest way!

"She's from Africa?" I asked, looking toward Yuzi, who was thankfully well on her way down the hall.

"Yes, and she smells like it," added Laney, wrinkling her nose. She handed me my lunch sack.

She didn't smell bad! I thought, but didn't have the nerve to say it. In fact, I think she was wearing some sort of berry body splash. She smelled great, actually! It would be a week before I learned that Yuzi wasn't even actually from Africa. She was born in **Texas**.

"Good luck at the pageant tonight," said Laney with a strange tone in her voice.

"But," protested Riley, "I thought you just said . . ."

Whatever Riley had wanted to say, Laney's icy glare stopped her in mid-sentence.

The two turned and walked away. Their little miniskirts swayed back and forth with major attitude.

The big yellow school bus bounced me the whole way home. I hoped that the shaking would help my little brainiac head find a creative way to tell my mom and dad about detention. When I finally arrived, I still didn't know what to say, and the ginormous mansion that everyone in town called McAllister Manor seemed big and frightening rather than warm and welcoming like usual. I reluctantly stepped toward the tall white marble columns that framed the two massive oak doors.

Fear evaporated completely when I pushed into the parlor, and my furry chocolate Labradoodle, Puddles, greeted me with a thumping tail. I patted him on the head and buried my face in his fluffy fur, squeezing his ears.

Feeling totally forgiven, if only by a four-legged creature, I headed straight for the kitchen. I was starved!

My mom was at the kitchen counter chopping up a tomato, but her eyes were red and puffy like they would be if she was carving up an onion. I could tell she'd been crying.

Nai Nai, my grandmother, was also there. She's not my real grandmother. She had been my foster mom when I was in the orphanage system in China eight years ago. Mom and Dad practically adopted her when they came to adopt me on my fourth birthday. They insisted she come with me. Since my dad buys lots of fireworks from companies in China, he had no trouble getting her a visa to come live with us.

Nai Nai was stirring a pot of chicken broth and was about to crack an egg into a bowl.

Oh no, I thought. *Egg drop soup! This can't be good.*

My grandmother thinks all of life's problems can be solved by a bowl of egg drop soup. She and Mom must have already heard about the Purple Flurp thing and detention.

"What's wrong, Mom?" I dared to ask.

"Oh, Danika," she said with a tenderness in her eyes. "Come here, baby."

She got up from the table and wrapped her arms around me for the longest time. That was certainly not the reaction I expected.

"I just spoke to Mrs. Butter," said Mom. "The Miss Teeny Pop committee heard about what happened at school. They think it would be better if you didn't compete tonight."

Dropping my bag full of books, I plopped down at the kitchen table and burst into tears.

"Eat soup," said Nai Nai suddenly, shoving a bowl in front of me and one in front of my mom. We just kept crying.

"*Eat* soup," insisted Nai Nai. "Soup make better." Nai Nai took my chin in her hands and made me look into her eyes. "I plllomise!"

Suddenly my tears turned into giggles. Nai Nai knew she could always make me laugh when she tried to say "promise."

Grabbing the spoon, I began to process the worst news **ever**.

"Mom," I said as she reached for her spoon to join me, "none of the routines we worked out will work with an odd number of contestants. They need ten of us."

Mom took my hand and looked me right in the eyes. "Danika, there's something else. The judges have asked Laney Douglas to take your place."

I guess who you sit with at lunch doesn't really mean that much after all.

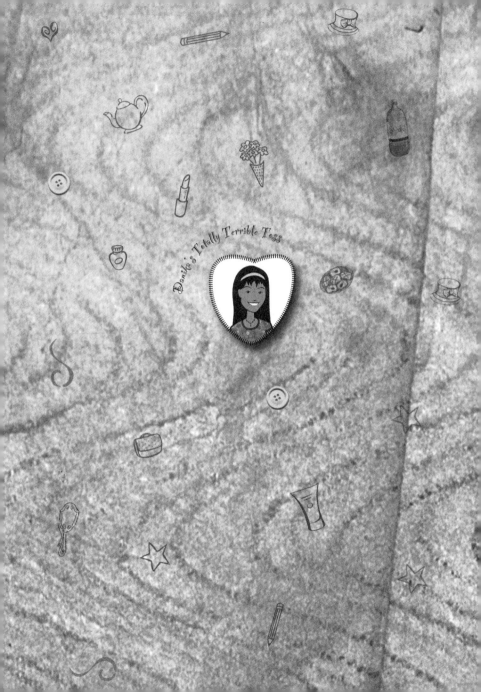

Danika's Totally Terrible Tess

CHAPTER 3

Pinky Promises

"Danika!"

Mom's voice floated up the spiral staircase into my bedroom suite and smacked me awake. I pulled the fluffy lime-green comforter up over my head and grumbled to myself, wishing the canopy on my bed was made out of soundproof glass rather than light pink tulle and bright green ribbons.

"Hurry out of bed, sweetheart." Her voice was muffled now since my ears were buried under four inches of fluff, but I could still hear her. "Your alarm went off fifteen minutes ago. I have leftover monkey bread from the Festival for breakfast."

Unpleasant memories of the past weekend flooded my barely awake cranium. Mom's Purple Flurp was more of a legend than ever. It was now responsible for making Popcorn Festival history *twice*! Once, just because it was delicious enough to win a popcorn cooking contest without having popcorn in it. Twice, because the judges of the Teeny Pop Pageant had disqualified me for throwing it at Mrs. Hefty. I had spent the entire weekend in my room with a box of tissues and my iPod. I had played every sad song Alayna Rayne had ever recorded at least two times an hour.

Ring-a-ling!

My white rhinestone-covered cell phone chirped to life. I reached for it, flipped it open, and pressed it to my ear without bothering to look at caller ID.

"Hello," I croaked and then cleared my throat.

"Danika!" The voice was familiar. Laney Douglas! Was she calling to rub in the fact that she'd replaced me?! I hadn't even bothered to check the paper to see if she had won Friday night, and Mom and Dad had been great about not bringing it up. "Did you hear?"

"Hear *what*?" I didn't hide how much this call annoyed me.

"We might both get to be in the Teeny Pop Pageant!" She sounded aflutter with happiness, and it was as genuine as the rhinestones on my cell phone.

"Huh?"

"We were all dressed for our first routine and waiting

backstage, when Mrs. Butter came out and announced that the recent disqualification and addition of contestants was being protested! *Protested*, Danika! They postponed the contest until the judges can get together and decide what to do. No one knows who started it all, but it must be someone really important for it to go down like that!"

"Snap!" I quipped.

"Massive snap!" said Laney.

Who could have possibly protested? I wondered to myself. I had a pretty good idea.

"Yeah, Laney. That's great news. I'll, uh, catch ya later!" I flipped my phone closed before she could respond.

Hopping from bed, I grabbed my grey minidress with orange flowers and a pair of black leggings. Mom always insists that I wear leggings with my miniskirts and short dresses. I ran a brush through my hair as fast as possible and plopped a bright orange headband over my black hair before slipping into my patent leather flats. I zoomed down the stairs.

"Dad!" I bellowed.

"Yes, my Beauty Queen?" He responded calmly, pulling his nose out of the newspaper. The headline on the front cover read: *Pageant Postponed!*

"Did you do *that*?" I asked, pointing to the black letters. It was just the kind of thing my dad would do. And he has power.

"I didn't say a word," he said calmly. "You must have a friend in high places."

I didn't know if I believed him.

After dinner that night, Mom loaded me into the BMW and insisted that we go visit the Hardings. Katie's dad is our pastor and Mom is super-good friends with Mrs. Harding, but Katie and I haven't been friends since fifth grade. I wasn't really excited about this.

Sitting awkwardly in the Hardings' living room and making small talk with Katie's mom was no fun at all. Finally, Katie showed up with her dad.

"Hey, Danika. Hi, Mrs. McAllister," she said when she walked in the front door.

Mrs. Harding looked at her and said, "Sweetie, why don't you and Danika go in your room and hang out for a bit while we talk?"

"Sure. Come on," invited Katie.

In her bedroom, I sat on Katie's blue fuzzy beanbag chairs. This was the exact spot where we'd traded stickers and dressed our Barbies countless times.

Since random thoughts were swirling through my head like a tornado, I couldn't really help it when one blurted out. "The Teeny Pop Pageant was **postponed** because of me."

"I heard," she answered sweetly. "I bet they'll let you back in."

"Did you hear why I was disqualified to begin with?" I asked.

"Danika, I was *there*," she said. "The *entire* sixth grade class was there." It didn't make me feel bad. She was just shooting straight with me. It made me miss our friendship.

"Everyone is saying that you stained Mrs. Hefty's face blue and that's why she's getting a week off. Is that true?" she asked.

"No! Of course not." I defended myself. "That's ridiculous! It was just my mom's totally awesome Purple Flurp. I've never even gotten a purple tongue from it!"

We both started giggling.

"So, I got a pink slip for it," I said quietly. "I have detention for three days this week with Mrs. V."

"No way!"

"Yes, way!"

"Me, too!"

Katie told me that she'd decided to declare her true
love for Zachary Donaldson on the bathroom walls.
My eyes must have been wide with how absolutely
unthinkable it was that my childhood Barbie-doll
buddy was now a graffiti artist.

"In *pencil*," she clarified. "So it could be erased.
Technically, that's not graffiti, is it?"

We laughed again.

"I got a pink eraser with *my* pink slip," she reported.
"Principal Butter had me totally erasing it today."

We both leaned back on the beanbags and stared up
at the glow-in-the-dark planet stickers on Katie's ceiling,
wondering what we should do. I said maybe there should
be a club for girls where they could tell all their secrets
and they could help each other not make stupid decisions.

I was kind of thinking out loud, but that sounded
like the seed of a great idea to Katie. Club names started
flooding my head, but they sounded really corny.

Suddenly, it hit me. I had a great idea. I knew exactly what we needed. I jumped up and said, "We'll call it the Secret Keeper Girl Club!"

"Like that really cool show our moms took us to a couple of years ago?" asked Katie.

"Yeah!" I said, jumping up and down. "That was the best night ever. Remember the helium saucer contest against our moms?"

"Yes, and they had great stories," added Katie.

"And the cool fashion show!"

Smiles stole across our faces and I got that feeling you get when you've laughed too much and your cheeks hurt.

"My favorite part was getting friendship bracelets," I said.

Katie moved over to her dresser where she opened a bright blue box. It kind of creaked when she opened it, then she reached in and pulled something out.

My eyes grew bright. It was our friendship bracelets. Katie still had them!

"Here's yours," she said, reaching out to tie mine onto my wrist. "You might recall we took them off at the beginning of fifth grade when we thought we were much too old to still wear friendship bracelets."

"Oh yeah," I sighed, wishing we had never taken them off. That's when Katie and I had first started growing apart.

I tied Katie's friendship bracelet on her. I thought about that night with the Secret Keeper Girl Tour team.

"Remember," I said, "that one teacher told us that in just a few years we'd really, really need our true friends to help us make good choices . . . and that it wouldn't be easy."

"Yeah," said Katie. "And that we needed a little circle of friends to share our deepest secrets with."

"I think we're in those years, Katie," I announced.

"Definitely," Katie agreed. "And, by the way, now that we're in those years, could you just call me Kate? I'm so over being called Katie!"

"Done," I said to my new—but at the same time old—best friend, Kate Harding.

"Pinky promise!" said Kate.

We linked pinkies and shook our hands up and down.

I had no idea that my promise of friendship would be tested the very next day.

Donita's Totally Terrible Toss

CHAPTER 4

Detention Deficit Disorder

Maybe Laney knows more about the pageant, I thought to myself. *I've got to know.*

I hadn't been in the cafeteria since I'd thrown the terribly imperfect Purple Flurp curve on Friday. I'd taken advantage of my school's outside lunch court passes, where basically all the kids trying to avoid someone in the cafeteria gather during warm, sunny days. I'd spent my last few lunch periods hanging out with people Laney could call losers. I could just see her making an "L" with her left hand and putting it up to her forehead.

But suddenly I couldn't stay out of the cafeteria. My desire to sit at the popular table completely took over. I felt like a moth flying toward one of those blue bug-zappers. I gave myself a quick pep talk on the way over to the table.

Maybe Laney would love Kate. Yep, I'm doing this for Kate. I'll bring her name up at the table and tell them how great she is. We'll take a vote and invite her to sit with us.

I took bold, deliberate steps toward the table.

"I'm back," I announced as I sat down.

No one said a word to me. Everyone looked at Laney.

"Hey," she finally said. "I hear the judges are still undecided."

"Oh, yeah?" I asked, ready to dig for the gold of more information.

Suddenly, Kate walked by. She didn't seem to notice me, but Riley saw her.

"*That* girl is boy crazy," said Riley, pointing shamelessly to Kate. "She even helped Toni Diaz sneak into the boys' locker room this week. I heard she likes every boy in sixth grade!"

"Oh, she doesn't like any of the sixth graders." I started to defend Kate. "She likes a *twelfth* grader. She even wrote his name . . ."

I stopped in mid-sentence, biting my lip. *What have I done?*

"She was the one who wrote Zachary Donaldson's name on the wall in the girls' bathroom!" said Laney, slamming her carton of milk down.

After it sank in, the whole table started laughing.

I was dreading my first detention because I didn't want to see Kate. What would she think if she knew I'd told her secret?

"Good afternoon, Danika," said Mrs. Velasquez as I walked into her art room to report for my first day of punishment. She's the absolute best. She lets us call her Mrs. V. I handed her my pink slip. She signed it and gave it back to me. "That clay pot you made in class on Monday is ready to be fired. Maybe you can help me load the kiln this afternoon."

"I'd love to," I answered. This was not what I thought detention would be like.

Kate was already seated, so I slipped in next to her and smiled weakly.

Next, a total tomboy-chick came in.

Oh yeah, I thought to myself. *She's probably the girl who dressed like a guy to try out for football last week.*

"Hello, Toni," said Mrs. V.

Toni Diaz! She's the girl Riley said was in the boys' locker room with Kate. That made perfect sense. Kate must have been helping her try out. That's so like Kate!

She said "hey" and took a seat.

Right behind her came that girl from Africa . . . Yuzi.

I'd heard that she was the one who pulled the fire alarm on Monday and created mass chaos. I smiled at her and waved like we were old friends.

Mrs. V encouraged us to read or work quietly. I pulled out my math homework because I had a ton of it. I'd started it in my study hall earlier in the afternoon.

"I hate math," I said, leaning over to Kate, trying to soothe my guilty conscience by just talking to her.

"You're great at math, Danika," Kate argued. "How can you hate it?"

"My homework is just totally messy."

"You need a sweet pencil," she answered.

"What?"

"I'll get you one," she said, reaching into her bag. "Sweet pencils make math sweet."

"Really? Thanks!" I said as I took the funky mechanical pencil with the bright pink pig topper on it.

Kate was right. Math did seem sweeter. Before I knew it, I had finished the last of my pre-algebraic challenges. As I pulled my three-ring binder open to insert my paper, I realized that I'd gotten so wrapped up in my math homework that

GO TO
secretkeepergirl.com
and type in the secret word
"Sweet" to create your
own sweet pencil!

I didn't notice that Kate had gone up to talk to Mrs. V.

"Hey, Danika! Come up and tell Mrs. V about the *Secret Keeper Girl Club!*"

Snapping my binder shut, I stood, then walked up to Mrs. V's desk.

"I don't really have it figured out," I said as Kate brushed past me with a notebook and a smile on her face.

"Well, let's see if I can help," she suggested gently. "What *do* you have?"

"A pretty messed-up life," I answered. A confession about Mrs. Hefty's Purple Flurp face mask dripped from my lips. Next, I told Mrs. V how Kate and I had made a pinky promise to be friends. Then I started to whisper. I told her how I'd sat with Laney today and told Kate's number one secret. She could tell I felt really bad.

"So, I have this idea for a club," I said, finally getting to the point of the conversation. "It'd be a club for girls where we could tell our deepest secrets. That's why we'd call it the *Secret Keeper Girl Club.*"

"Sounds like a good idea, Danika," she said, sitting down behind her desk. "I have something I want to give to you."

Her metal school desk creaked when she opened a side drawer. She reached into it, then placed a super fancy pen

43

in front of me. It was made of pinkish-colored marble and had a frilly, white feathery thing on top.

"It's the sweetest of all sweet pens," she said, mimicking Kate's super cool voice. Then she continued in her regular voice. "It's a fountain pen. I got it when I was crowned Miss Teeny Pop."

My mouth dropped open. "You were Miss Teeny Pop?"

"Thirteen years ago," said Mrs. V.

"Wow!" I said, picking the pen up for a closer look. "Thanks!" The desire to be Miss Teeny Pop grew to gargantuan proportions at that very moment. I wanted it more than ever. No wonder Mrs. V was considered the coolest teacher at Rutherford B. Hayes.

"You need club rules," explained Mrs. V. "I'm giving you my pen to write them all down."

She pulled out a large sheet of bright yellow paper, folded it in half, opened it, and pushed it across the table to me. "You can write them here."

"How do I know what to write?"

"You find out what it takes to be a true friend, Danika."

I just looked at her blankly. So she continued.

"Can I risk sounding like a teacher?"

I nodded.

"There's an old proverb about friendship that I like a lot. It says, 'Become wise by walking with the wise, but hang out with fools and watch your life fall to pieces!'"

Between detention and watching my dream to be Miss Teeny Pop teetering on the brink of disaster, I was pretty sure my life was falling to pieces.

"You want friends who are wise or, well . . . smart, but not in an 'I got an A in algebra' kind of way. Friends who think with you to make good decisions! And that makes you a good friend, because you are wise enough to help them think, too."

This was making sense. Kate and I had talked about helping each other not to write on bathroom walls and throw Purple Flurp!

"Anyway," she continued with a smile, "all you need to worry about now is finding the path to true friendship. So, you are going to need to take a few walks like the proverb says. After each walk, you'll know what the next rule of the *Secret Keeper Girl Club* is going to be."

"OK," I said. "I think I get it. Who do I walk with first?"

"You might think about where your feet took you today at lunch," she answered. "You seem to be feeling pretty bad for telling Kate's secret. What did that teach you?"

I didn't have to think long. I leaned over on her desk and wrote:

RULE #1: Always keep each other's secrets!

Mrs. V was smiling when I looked up.

"You have your first rule!" she said, offering me a high five. We slapped hands.

Mrs. V talked to me about how important it is to keep each other's secrets, but told me all about how I needed to talk to my mom if a secret seemed to be dangerous for me or my friend. I rolled my eyes a little bit because she sounded just like my mom. Mom is always telling me all that "stranger-danger" kind of stuff.

That's when I realized that Mrs. V might be the coolest teacher on the planet, but she's still a teacher. We sat there just looking at each other and I knew she loved me kind of like my mom does. It was a little weird so I had to break the silence!

"But it's just Kate and me, and that's not much of a club," I said.

We sat there for just a moment. Then, Mrs. V leaned over her table and started to whisper. Her eyes were bright and she looked like a sixth grader herself.

"You know, there are four girls in this room. I bet you and Kate aren't the only ones who wished they had a club of friends."

I looked back and Toni and Yuzi had their eyes locked in a gaze that was aimed our way. Even so, they looked like they hadn't understood that Mrs. V was talking about them. I reflexively averted my gaze from them, pretending like I wasn't looking at them. I just hate it when people do that!

"Danika," whispered Mrs. V again, "Yuzi is new to town. I can only imagine how much she must need friends right now. I hear her family is African, she was born in Texas, and she just moved here from London. What stories she must have to tell!"

I looked back again. Yuzi had a bright-eyed innocence about her. She smiled at me. I smiled back. At that moment, I just wanted to go hug her.

I excitedly motioned for Kate to come back up, and the three of us whispered for a while.

"Toni is in a tough place, too," offered Kate. "She told me she'd dreamed of playing football since as long as she can remember walking! But her mom and dad have said **'no way'** and she's in a lot of trouble for trying out anyway.

She's lost her dream."

I knew how that felt.

"Let's do it," I said. "Let's ask Toni and Yuzi to be in the club, too!"

Kate didn't actually answer, but her squeal of delight told me she was in agreement with Mrs. V and me.

We walked right over to Toni and Yuzi and asked if they wanted to be part of our brand-new *Secret Keeper Girl Club*.

They seemed a little shocked by the invitation.

"Yes," Yuzi blurted. Then louder, "Yes. I'll do it."

"I'm in," said Toni.

Everyone smiled so big I thought their faces might burst.

"You can meet in my room on Wednesdays," said Mrs. V.

Excited chatter exploded among the girls, and Mrs. V pulled me aside.

"You'll know who to walk with next," she said. "It'll be pretty clear to you when you figure out what you need to do to protect rule number one."

I didn't even have to think about it. I knew exactly who I was supposed to "walk with" next, but I was totally terrified.

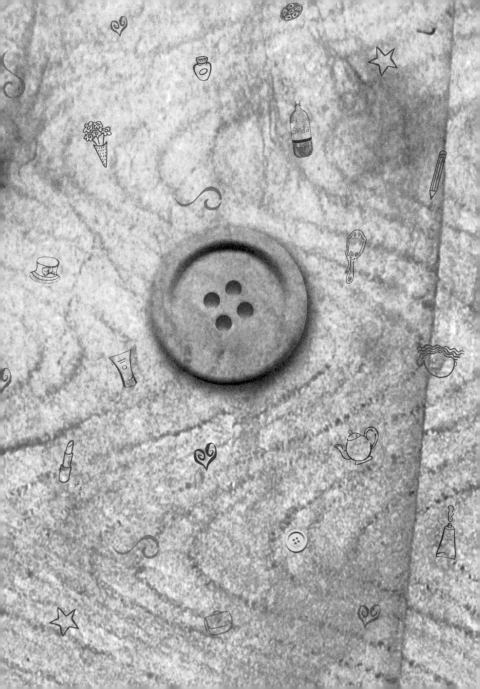

Danika's Totally Terrible Tess

CHAPTER 5

No Boys Allowed

"Dani." My dad's voice woke me. He's the only one who's never called me Danika. It's always been Dani. "Wake up, Beauty Queen!" He's the only one who calls me that, too.

"There's something interesting in the paper," he said in a teasing tone, and I could feel him flop down on my bed. I heard the paper rattling around on top of the covers.

"Oh, Daddy," I complained, stuffing my head under my puffy lime-green comforter. "Since when do I read the paper?"

"When it's about the Teeny Pop contest," he said.

I sat up straight as an arrow, looked down at my lap, and grabbed the *Marion Star*. The front-page headline read, "Pageant Plans Popped!" I started to read out loud as fast as possible:

> In a controversial turn of events, the Teeny Pop Pageant was postponed last Friday night, making Popcorn Festival history. An unnamed contestant was disqualified due to what is being termed a public disturbance.

"Public disturbance!? Oh, brother!" I whined, but quickly got back to my reading.

After the young woman had been disqualified, a member of the Festival committee came forward to protest and the contest was delayed. The name of the committee member is still being withheld, but based on the person's testimony it is believed that the incident involving the young woman in question was overblown.

I sure wanted to know who said that! It *must've* been Dad. I started skimming down to the paragraph with the contestants' names. I read them out loud:

Abbey Anderson
Kylie Burger
Autumn Clouderton
Laney Douglas
Julia Donaldson
Morgan Gray
Lindsay Hermana
Shannon Latchman
Lexi Livingstone
Kimberly Marion
Danika McAllister

"Danika McAllister!" I screeched out a second time and bounced my body up and down on the bed. "Wait! Dad, there's one more name."

Riley Peterson

"Riley Peterson!?" I repeated, looking at my dad like the world had just turned upside down.

But I decided quickly that it was my new best-day-ever and I didn't complain. In no time at all, I was headed out the door to enjoy the pleasure of walking the halls of Rutherford B. Hayes as an un-disqualified Teeny Pop contestant.

"No need soup today," called Nai Nai behind me as I walked to the bus stop.

Having recently just had a no-good, awful day complete with Purple Flurp fiasco, my best-day-ever felt really perfect. I even had the courage to face what I needed to do to protect *Secret Keeper Girl Club* rule number one: Always keep each other's secrets.

I sat under the big maple tree in the front of the school waiting for Kate, who'd agreed to meet me for lunch. We had both requested outside lunch court passes for today! Secretly, I think Mrs. V told Principal Butter that Kate and I needed to talk. How else would two girls who just got pink slips have gotten lunch court passes? My mini cucumber on rye sandwiches were stacked into a tall tower on my books. I was concentrating on balancing a green grape on top of the magnificent work of art when some-one covered my eyes. I felt the sandwiches scatter.

"Sorry," Kate said. "I've got . . ." She fumbled around in her brown sack. ". . . egg salad by the smell of it. Trade?"

"Sure!" I said. "You can have my orange crème soda, too."

"Whoa!" Kate bellowed. "Call in the paramedics! Do you have a fever?" She touched my forehead and looked at me with exaggerated concern. "Nothing . . . no nothing ever comes between Danika McAllister and her orange crème sodas. 'Sup?"

She crunched down on the first bite of her cucumber sandwich and waited for me to answer. There was no easy way to say it, so I just went for it.

"Yesterday at lunch, I told Laney Douglas and her whole stupid fan club that you like a twelfth grader," I confessed as fast as possible.

Kate's mouth gaped open and her mash of rye, cream cheese, and cukes looked like it might spill out of her mouth.

"I did not tell her who!" I said defensively. Then I realized

54

I had nothing to defend and I added softly, "I think they figured it out, though."

Kate started chewing again real fast. "No big deal!" she said. But I knew she didn't mean it. She got those red blotches on her neck that she gets when she's real mad, like when her cat Sharkey wouldn't come down out of the tree for six hours. She was definitely, 100%, over-the-top ticked. And she should be.

"I'm sorry," I said. "I know I'm the worst best friend ever and the last person on earth who should start the *Secret Keeper Girl Club*. I don't even know how to be a good friend."

"No, it really is OK," said Kate. "I mean, it's not cool . . . what you did, but it's totally cool that you told me. I forgive you."

I sighed in relief.

"What can I do to make it up to you?" I asked.

"Well, you do owe me," she said. We both leaned back into the grass to think, looking up at the huge orange leaves on the maple tree.

"I know," she said, sitting up. "The first club rule is really about what you need to be a good friend. I mean, no offense, but you could have used that rule yesterday at lunch. Anyway,

I totally have a rule to propose for our club that'll help me. I'm really trying to sort out something about boys."

Kate opened up to me that she was really, completely obsessed with Zachary Donaldson and that she got the sense that her parents were not sure what to do about it. Mrs. V had been giving her secret assignments to figure out guys. After taking it all in, it sounded to me like Kate's heart was kind of messed up when it came to boys. At that moment, I was kind of glad my dad had a strict "no boys" policy!

"I have a rule," said Kate. "Anyone who is in an all-girls club knows that this should be the uber-rule."

"Uber isn't even a word," I said.

"Yes, it is. It means super," Kate said defiantly.

"Then why not just say super?"

"Because uber means super-duper, but doesn't sound totally dorky."

"Hold it!" I demanded.

Kate stopped chewing and looked at me again.

"What's the rule?" I asked.

"No boys allowed!" said Kate.

In Mrs. V's detention, I told Toni and Yuzi about the stupid thing I did to offend Rule #1 and how Kate's the coolest friend ever because she forgave me. Then I told them Kate's uber-rule. They agreed that it's a good rule and we made it Rule #2 with special uber-status not to be confused with the importance of Rule #1. I took out my sweet pen and yellow paper and wrote it down:

RULE #2: No boys allowed

Kate took a tube of lip gloss from the pocket of her sweatshirt and slid the wand across her lips. When she smacked her lips, it smelled good.

"What's that scent?" asked Toni. "It's great!"

"Banana berry! It's my fave!"

"Can I propose a rule?" asked Yuzi, and continued without waiting for an answer. "Rule #3: Banana berry is the official club flavor for lip gloss."

Everyone giggled, but I pulled out my pen to write.

RULE #3: Only wear banana berry flavored lip gloss!

"Good rules," said Mrs. V a few minutes later as I helped her unload the pottery kiln we loaded yesterday. "I'm really proud of you. You did what you needed to do to protect

Rule #1, and it gave Kate the courage to begin to talk about where she needs help in her life. That's what it means to 'walk with the wise.'"

"Thanks, Mrs. V," I said, taking another pot from her and putting it on the shelf behind me.

"If someone is obsessed with someone or something, they usually need help getting over it," she said.

"You know, my Nai Nai needs some help with her obsession for egg drop soup," I said, laughing. I told her about how Nai Nai is always shoving another bowl in front of whichever one of us in the house has had a bad day. Mrs. V just nodded and listened.

"Have you ever asked her why she makes egg drop soup?" said Mrs. V. "Maybe there's a secret to it. Maybe it really does help when you're having a bad day."

I just laughed.

"Do you think your grandmother is wise?" she asked.

I still wasn't getting the whole "wise" thing.

"Does she help you make good decisions?" Mrs. V clarified.

"Well, sure," I said. "I guess so."

"Maybe you've just uncovered the next person you need to walk with," said Mrs. V.

I can't believe I'm actually going to ask my ancient Chinese grandma for a Secret Keeper Girl rule, but it's worth a shot.

Danika's Totally Terrible Toss

CHAPTER 6

The Egg Drop Soup Slurp

As soon as the bell rang for lunch, I sprinted for my locker and then out to the patch of soft, green grass under the maple tree. Fear of facing Laney and Riley kept me out of the cafeteria. I figured Kate shouldn't have to face them either, so the whole club got outside lunch court passes.

Toni and Yuzi ran up together just as my mom's BMW pulled up to the curb. Nai Nai stepped out from the passenger's side, walked to the trunk, and retrieved a tray covered in red fabric. Anything covered in red is important to her. She took a few minutes arranging things and then proudly walked toward us while Mom drove away.

"Hey, Nai Nai," said Kate, who was just arriving. "Can I help you with that?"

Kate took the load and Nai Nai pulled back the red covering to reveal five bottles of orange crème soda and five huge bowls of steaming egg drop soup. My grandmother carefully sprinkled some green scallions on the top, along with her special homemade fried wonton noodles. Then she passed everything out.

We were all carefully balancing our bowls when Nai Nai bowed her head. We bowed ours, too, but Nai Nai didn't say anything out loud.

"Amen!" she said in her thick Chinese accent.

"No tell secret of soup now," she said, getting right down to business. "First, we eat and speak."

Nai Nai slurped her soup loudly. Toni and Yuzi's eyes grew wide, so Kate picked up her bowl and totally out-slurped my grandma. Kate rocks! We all started slurping, and the soup was way too delicious for us to laugh at how silly we sounded.

I knew what Nai Nai was going to say next, but she didn't say it. She just looked at me and nodded as if I should take it from here. Nai Nai always asks me the same two questions when we eat egg drop soup.

"So," I started, "the first question to answer when eating Nai Nai's egg drop soup is 'What is the worst thing about your day?'"

Before I could go on I heard a guy's voice yelling. "Heads up, Da-neeka!"

I knew that voice! I looked up and saw a soccer ball hurling toward our little circle. Yuzi shrieked and the ball dropped into the circle, nearly knocking over my soup.

"Chad-the-dork Ferner!" I shouted. "You did that on purpose."

"Maybe I did. Maybe I didn't," he said, tugging on my ponytail as he retrieved the ball. He ran off before I could hit him.

Ugh!

"You wanna hear an answer to 'What's the worst thing about your day?'" I said. "Mine is Chad Ferner!"

Nai Nai giggled.

"I think you best thing in his day," she said.

My girlfriends erupted into laughter. When everyone calmed down, Yuzi piped up, "The worst thing about my day every day this week is that I'm the new girl who everyone thinks is the bad girl. I did not pull that fire alarm on Monday morning and I'm going to prove it. It feels really lousy walking through the hall and getting called names!"

We were all quiet.

"Well, I wasn't going to tell anyone this," Kate suddenly jumped in. "But I don't want Yuzi to think she's all alone. Laney and Riley have been in my face about the Zachary Donaldson thing."

I felt totally bad and I wanted to say something, but I didn't get a chance before Toni jumped in.

"That's so mean!" she said. "Today I walked by Trevor Kenworth and he yelled, 'Look out! Tree comin' through!' just to be stupid."

Toni's really tall for a sixth-grade girl.

"He's just jealous because you're more of an athlete than he is," said Kate. "Don't let him get to you."

"And Yuzi," said Toni, "we love you!" Everyone smiled and Toni wrapped her arms around Yuzi's neck while precariously balancing her egg drop soup on one knee.

"Velly good!" said Nai Nai. I was glad no one made fun of how she said "very." She nodded at me again.

"The next question is always, 'What's the best thing about your day?' I'll start. You might think the best thing about my day is getting invited back into the Teeny Pop Contest, but it's not. The best thing is that Kate forgave me and is having lunch with me."

Kate, who was seated right next to me, leaned in and

gave me a side hug. Then she said, "The best thing about my day was going to be that I'm going to get to see Zachary Donaldson play football tonight, but . . ."

We all groan.

"No boys allowed," teased Toni.

"OK, the best thing so far is this soup!" said Kate.

Nai Nai smiled so hard that her eyes turned into little tiny slits and I couldn't see her eyeballs. I sure could see her teeth though!

"The best thing for me is detention and we didn't even have it yet," said Toni. "It's been the best part of every day for me since it started. I can't believe how much fun we're having."

We all agreed.

"Don't tell Principal Butter!" Yuzi giggled. "Hmmmm. Let's see. The best thing about my day was waking up and knowing I have three new friends and we're going to be in a club together."

This time, I reached over and hugged Yuzi. She just sighed and smiled.

Nai Nai was cleaning up the bowls.

"We done," she said abruptly.

"But Nai Nai," I complained. "You didn't tell us the secret.

You told us that if we talked, you'd tell us the secret of the soup."

"Secret not in soup," she said. "It in you." She pointed to my heart. "Soup just make you slow down!"

I got it!

"Eating egg drop soup is like chilling," I said. "You know, slowing down to figure it all out. The good and the bad."

It sure is easy to feel the bad, I thought. *But I guess there's always some good to go with it.*

Slowing down to eat the soup made us all feel better. We suddenly didn't feel alone in our problems. We talked about it while Nai Nai stood there waiting for Mom to pick her up. Toni said we should make egg drop soup the official food of the *Secret Keeper Girl Club* and that we should eat a lot of it. We all agreed. I took out my sweet pen and yellow paper and wrote:

RULE #4: Eat a lot of Egg Drop Soup!

Just as the lunch bell rang, Principal Butter and Mrs. Butter walked past us.

"Congratulations, Danika," said Mrs. Butter, waving as she walked by in her high heels, lemon-yellow dress suit, and matching pillbox hat. She and Principal Butter were two peas in a pod. A pod from 1955! "We were pulling for you," she said cheerfully.

I can't believe she just said that. I'm sure I stood about a half a foot taller. It was the highest compliment I'd ever gotten.

67

"Be sure to go over your rules carefully," she said. "The new judges have all been instructed to be really picky due to the week they've just had of parents calling and fussing about this or that. By the way, thank your parents. They never called and they sure had a right to."

So my dad really *wasn't* the one who rescued me! Then who was it?

Danika's Totally Terrible Tags

CHAPTER 7

Cinderella and the Ugly Stepsister

On Saturday morning when I pried my eyes open, the clock read 10:19. Wow! I'd slept for twelve straight hours!

I decided to put on a simple pair of light blue skinny jeans with my black Audrey Hepburn T-shirt. I don't really know who Audrey Hepburn is, but Mom says she was a great actress. I just like the T-shirt. I slipped my hair into a ponytail and wondered what kind of Saturday morning chores my mom would insist I complete. Housekeeper and personal assistant aside, my mom always has **chores** for me to do on Saturdays!

She must have heard me moving around.

"Danika." Her voice broke through my thoughts. "I have something I need you to do!"

Big surprise, I thought.

I trudged down the spiral staircase to our front foyer with the big marble columns and patted Puddles on the head. She always greets us with a thumping tail every morning. I love that.

I sniffed the air and detected pancakes.

"Dani," Dad said, placing his hand on my head. "Your mom makes the best flapjacks in the world. I just gained ten pounds eating them. But I'm sorry. There are none left for sleepyheads!"

"Dad!" I moaned, knowing full well that Mom would have some for me and that she'd add bananas and whipped topping to them. Just then Mom turned. Sure enough, she had a plateful just like I liked 'em.

"Danika, this morning your chores are easy," she said, placing the plate in front of me. "Walk Puddles and try on that Teeny Pop dress!"

"Again?" I questioned. "My body hasn't changed in one week, Mom! We don't need to fit the dress again, do we?"

"If you'd rather, I can write a list of other chores," she said. I knew the list would likely include scrubbing toilets, giving Puddles a bath, or dusting Mom's entire collection of imported china. I was up for the dress fitting!

"You are beautiful, my princess," said Mom as I modeled my Teeny Pop Pageant ball gown. "I'm so happy that you're going to get to wear this. You know, your dad and I are so proud of how you just waited the system out and didn't fight. It all worked out because you had a good heart! Twirl!"

"Mom!" I begged.

"Please!" she begged back.

I reluctantly twirled. My dress is so amazing that it looked like the best twirl in all of dress-twirling history. It's light blue and has a fitted satin top with sequins and pearls hand-sewn into it. The skirt is a full, billowy bundle of tulle. It's a one of a kind. Mom had a designer make my dress since it's my last year in the Teeny Pop contest. I love it. It reminds me of the dress from Cinderella. That's the most beautiful dress in the world. Mine is second-most beautiful. It passes all of the pageant dress rules:

It's one solid color.

It has a full, ballroom skirt. (We're not allowed to have fitted ones.)

It's got sleeves. (We're not allowed to have off-the-shoulder or strapless dresses.)

"I love it, Mom," I said. "Thanks! Even if I don't win, I'm going to have a blast!" It's the first time I've admitted I might not win.

"Danika," she said, "do you want to talk about it?"

"No," I said, but then remembered that Mrs. V had given me another "walking" assignment. "But would you want to walk with me and Puddles?"

She smiled.

After I took my dress off, she grabbed her white cable-knit sweater and I grabbed my new black Rutherford B. Hayes Middle School sweatshirt. Puddles knew we were going for a walk and stood at the door sideways banging her tail against the wall. It seemed to me that banging a body part against the wall like that might hurt, but she looked happy enough. I clicked her leash onto her collar and headed out the door.

"Mom, I need to ask you a question," I said. She already knew about Laney, and her response was that she's delighted about me being friends with Kate and starting the club. I filled her in on Mrs. V's assignments and the list of club rules so she'd have all the facts before I asked the question.

"He who walks with the wise grows wise," she said. "I know that proverb. It's in the Bible. It's one of my favorite verses. What's your question?"

"My question is this: How do you know who's a wise friend? Do they have to be old to be wise?" I asked.

"I don't think so," said Mom. "Some old people are just old. They've never grown into wise friends."

"Are they wise if they ace every test?"

"That just makes 'em smart, don't you think? There's a difference between smart and wise!" She took Puddles from me because a bunny ran across the street. She'll chase bunnies. Not my mom, Puddles.

"One of my favorite quotes is from an old dead guy," Mom said. She has a way of bringing things to my level. I think that's why my friends love her. "I can't remember his name. Emerson or Ralph or something. Famous, though! Anyway, he said 'Real friendship is shown in times of trouble; prosperity is full of friends.'"*

"Huh?" I said. I may be a straight-A student, but that went way over my head. "Say again?"

"Wise friends stick around even when things aren't going great. That's why I think that your friendship club is so great. It sounds like it all started when the four of you got into trouble and had to do detention together. I'm thinkin' that girls who want to use that kind of a bad experience to start a true friendship club are the kinds of girls I want you to be friends with."

I was happy to hear that my mom was proud of me.

*Ralph Waldo Emerson

"Yeah, it's cool!" I said.

"Foolish friends are only around for the party. Watch out for them."

"Got it!" I said.

I was just about to crawl under my comfy covers when I heard my cell phone beep. I'd gotten a text message.

U up?

The phone zipped out of my hands when I realized the text was from Laney Douglas. It took me a moment to realize that I'd thrown it. It was one of those "Ew! It's a bug!" kind of responses.

I picked the phone up like it was a bomb about to explode and typed:

IDK

IDK? I don't know if I'm up? How dumb is that, I thought. I pushed the send button, anyway.

My phone rang almost immediately.

"Sup, Danika." I never noticed how nasal Laney's voice was.

"Me, I guess," I said. "What's up with you, Laney?" I said it nicely, but I think she understood we were on shaky ground.

"Like, I just didn't want you to think I had anything to do with the whole pageant problem. I'm real sorry about that.

But it's working out, so that's good . . ." She waited for me to respond, but I didn't want to say anything mean, and I didn't have anything nice to say.

"Anyway, Riley and I are here hanging."

"Hey!" said Riley.

"Hey," I said flatly, realizing for the first time that she rarely spoke unless Laney gave her the green light.

"Anyway," continued Laney. "We just realized something. We totally have a good shot at getting those front row seats to the Alayna Rayne concert. There are three of us in the pageant and you *know* one of us is going to win. The winner gets four tickets and there are, like, only three of us."

Wow! Laney can add, I said to myself as she babbled on.

"So, if we all make a pact to take each other if we win, then we'll pretty much for sure get to go."

Suddenly I understood why Laney Douglas would want to be in the pageant she had made fun of for as long as I can remember. She was just like that lady in Florida who stood by a statue of Alayna Rayne for six days without sleeping or showering to win two tickets and a backstage pass. This was just a silly celebrity concert contest to Laney. Maybe Riley, too.

"Ummm, Danika," said Laney. "Are you there or what?"

"I'm here," I said impatiently. "I just have to think about that offer." I needed to get some advice from my Secret Keeper Girl buds, but I was pretty sure the answer was going to be a loud "**No!**"

"Well, OK," Laney said, sounding shocked that anyone wouldn't just say yes to her every desire. "Like, well, I'm wearing a pink ballroom dress in the contest. What color is yours?"

"Look, Laney, I've really got to get to bed," I said. "Could we talk about this another time?" *Like never?*

"OK, see ya at lunch!" she said and her phone clicked off.

I snapped mine shut.

Is it possible that Laney Douglas just invited me back to the popular table just to win tickets to the Alayna Rayne concert?

Donita's Totally Terrible Togs

CHAPTER 8

A Hefty Surprise

By Tuesday at lunch, it had gotten around that Toni Diaz had tried out to be the school's Shark mascot and failed miserably. She was obviously embarrassed.

"Don't feel bad," Yuzi said as we sat under the maple tree again, feasting on our PB&J and other all-American lunch food. "You should have seen what happened to *me* in a costume!" She told us how her mom had volunteered her to dress up as a cob of corn during the Popcorn Festival and how she'd wiped out in the thing big time.

"Oh, wow!" I said. "That was *my* costume! My dad's ad agency made it for me to wear in last year's Teeny Pop contest. It was for my commercial presentation. I represented Orville Redenbacher popcorn."

"OK," quipped Yuzi. "I totally dislike you right now!" I knew she was kidding.

"There needs to be a club rule about costumes," suggested Kate.

"Yeah, like *no* costumes," said Toni.

"Especially produce," added Yuzi.

I pulled out my sweet pen and started writing.

That afternoon I couldn't wait to get to Mrs. V's classroom for our first club meeting. When Toni finally showed up a little late, I called the first Secret Keeper Club meeting to order.

"Ahem." I cleared my throat to sound official. "May I present to you Danika, Kate, Toni, and Yuzi's *Secret Keeper Girl Club* Rules." My mom had helped me design them in a really cool computer program and I had updated it during my last period study hall, so all of our rules so far were on it. I presented each girl and Mrs. V with a copy of the rules.

Danika, Kate, Toni, and Yuzi's Secret Keeper Girl Club Rules

RULE #1: Always keep each other's secrets!

RULE #2: No boys allowed!

RULE #3: Only wear banana berry flavored lip gloss.

RULE #4: Eat a lot of egg drop soup.

RULE #5: Wise friends stand beside each other through tough times. Foolish ones just come to the parties. Be there!

RULE #6: No costumes ever . . . especially produce.

I was so proud of our club rules.

"I have a gift for everyone," said Kate. She pulled five tubes of lip gloss out of her backpack. "It's banana berry!" We all tried ours on right away, including Mrs. V.

"I also have something, but just for Toni and Yuzi," said Mrs. V. She opened her hand and I couldn't believe it. She had two friendship bracelets just like the ones Kate and I got at the Secret Keeper Girl event two years ago.

"Wow!" I said. "Where did you get those?"

"Oh, I have my connections!" she said.

We all looked at her, silently begging for more.

"It's called the Internet!" she explained. "Secret Keeper Girl has a cool Web site and I got on, emailed them, and asked for two more bracelets!"

"Cool!" said Toni.

"You might check it out," she said. "It actually has ideas for how to start a *Secret Keeper Girl Club*."

"We're not the only ones?" Yuzi asked.

"Apparently not!" said Mrs. V.

"Uber-cool!" said Kate.

"Danika, come on over here," called Mrs. V after we helped Toni and Yuzi tie their bracelets onto their wrists. "I've got something else for you."

"What?"

"I think I have another walk for you. It'll be your last one. Any club rules you come up with after this one are all from you. But I think there's someone wise you should talk to." She was being awfully mysterious.

"Who?"

"The first ever Miss Teeny Pop!" she said.

"She's alive?"

"Oh my! Yes!" Mrs. V laughed. "She's only forty years old. She's got a lot of life in her. In fact, she's got a lot of fight in her, and she's been using it these past two weeks to get you back into the Teeny Pop contest!"

I couldn't believe it. I was going to find out who helped me!

Mrs. V pulled out a newspaper, yellowed with age. It was an old *Marion Star*—twenty-four years old. The front cover had a big black-and-white photograph of the first ever Miss Teeny Pop. She was petite and had long blonde hair. She was wearing a beautiful dress. *That's the third-most beautiful dress in the world,* I thought to myself.

I took the paper in my hand and just stared into her eyes. They looked oddly familiar.

"Angela Moody," I said, reading her name.

"You'll find her at this address," said Mrs. V, handing me a Post-it. "It's right around the corner from the school. And I happen to know she's there right now."

"Really," I said, looking up at the clock on the wall. I had forty-five minutes until my mom picked me up. "Gotta go, Secret Keeper sistas! Bye!"

"117 Hayes Avenue."

A fall breeze almost blew the Post-it from my hand as I peeked at it. Comparing Mrs. V's handwritten address to the number on the little yellow house, I scanned the white picket fence for a way inside the yard. There was a gate under a big white arch. I pushed it open and walked through the aisle of mums in full bloom. The porch was as old-fashioned as they come. Kind of cozy compared to my mammoth house. I liked it. I pushed the little round button next to the door and heard the doorbell buzz.

At first, no one came.

I started to get nervous and thought to myself that I should just turn and run.

Before I could, I saw the form of someone just inside the frosted window of the door. It was someone rather big. Maybe it was the first Miss Teeny Pop's husband.

It sure couldn't be the petite little lady I'd seen in the paper clipping.

I saw the door handle turn, and the door opened quickly.

"*Mrs. Hefty?*" I asked. I stood there in shock before I had the guts to ask, "How are you?"

"Oh fine, dear," she said. "Come on in." Pushing the screen door open, she wiped her hands on her bright floral apron. She had on a yellow T-shirt and jeans. And her hair wasn't pressed against her head by a net. It flowed loosely around her shoulders. She looked so much younger when she wasn't in her uniform.

"Umm," I stammered, "I think I must be at the wrong place. Does Angela Moody live here?"

"You're lookin' at her," said Mrs. Hefty, and then she started rambling just like she did in the cafeteria, but I liked it. A lot. "It's Angela Hefty now, I'm afraid. Put up with being Moody my whole life only to get it exchanged for Hefty. Oh, dear! Well, Mrs. V said you might stop by and I took the liberty of making some of my Monster Cookies. Huge things, they are. Everything in the world in them. It takes two spatulas to get those puppies off the pan. But it doesn't take two *Mr.* Heftys to eat them."

I followed her into the kitchen. There was a glass bottle of milk from Young's Dairy on the old-fashioned dining room table, and two plates filled with the biggest cookies I'd ever seen in my life. We sat down and started eating as Mrs. Hefty told me all kinds of tales about winning the Miss Teeny Pop crown. Then she told me how she'd almost single-handedly gotten me back into the contest.

"I knew ya didn't mean it, Miss McAllister!" she said. "I knew that day when it happened that you were just caught up in the same peer pressure I felt when I was in sixth grade. It's not fun. Everyone feels pressure to sit next to certain people in the lunchroom!"

"You *know* about that?" I asked in wonder, thinking she must be the only adult who knows about the number one rule to surviving middle school.

"I work in the cafeteria, my dear," she said and giggled. "And, Danika, you were sitting with the *wrong* girls the day I had my first taste of Purple Flurp."

"Sorry," I said shyly.

"Apology accepted," she said.

"Did you really have to take the week off because your face turned blue from it?" I inquired. I just had to know.

Mrs. Hefty giggled. "My dear, of course not. That's the silliest thing I've ever heard. Oh my, my, my. No. Truth is . . . it took a lot of time to get those judges turned around. Principal Butter and I both felt so bad about how things got blown up that we agreed I should take the week to fix our . . . ah . . . little Purple Flurp fiasco! Fact is, I thought it a tasty treat, though I'd rather have it in my mouth than on my chin!" She laughed at her own joke and I promised to get mom to make her a batch so she could eat it. She asked me to bring it to the Teeny Pop Pageant tomorrow night.

"You'll be there?" I asked.

"Haven't missed it in twenty-four years," she said. "Let me show you two things before you leave, Danika. This way. Follow me. There we go!"

She took me into a tiny little den and stood me in front of a big-framed quote. It read: *The only way to have a friend is to be one.*" Ralph Waldo Emerson.

"That's my favorite quote," said Mrs. Hefty. "Mrs. V says you've been thinking a lot about friendship. That about sums it up for me."

No lecture. Just a quote. You didn't have to be a rocket scientist to understand it, either. I instantly realized then that I spent way too much middle-school energy worrying about who liked me and not enough looking for who *needed* me. I understood then that Mrs. Hefty was one of my best friends. She was there when I needed her. I decided then and there that we needed to add another rule to our Secret Keeper Girl Club and it would be that quote! I imagined myself writing it onto the list:

RULE #7: Be a friend. It's the only way to have one!

"One more thing," she said, opening a trunk next to a well-worn olive-green La-Z-Boy. She lifted a crown from the top of the pile inside. I was surprised that it was pretty much just plastic and it was bent up a lot. She placed it on my head. When I turned to look at her, the crown fell off, and she put it back in the trunk.

"Crowns get stuck in trunks, Danika," she said. "Friends last a whole lot longer. *Be* one."

I wasn't sure what she meant, but in the next twenty-four hours it would become very clear to me.

Darla's Totally Terrible Toss

CHAPTER 9

Breaking the Rules . . . Again!

"Laney, I can't do it!" I said.

Finally standing backstage at the Teeny Pop Pageant, I found myself once again face-to-face with Laney Douglas's impertinent whining. The curtain was about to come up for the choreographed group opening, and she was still pressuring me to agree to sharing the Alayna Rayne tickets if I won.

"*If* I win, I'm going to take my best friends: Kate, Toni, and Yuzi." Through a slit in the curtain I could see them seated in the front row with my mom, dad, Nai Nai, Mrs. Hefty, and Mrs. V. I had my very own fan club!

The music started and Laney huffed over to her position, stomping all the way in her chartreuse dress suit and black patent leather ballerina slippers. She looked like a four-year-old who didn't get the Barbie she wanted. I realized that she looked like that a lot, but this was the moment I'd been waiting for, and nothing was going to ruffle my feathers.

"Ladies and gentlemen, your contestants for this year's Miss Teeny Pop!" That was our cue. I took the deepest breath ever, straightened my white-sequined headband, and checked to make sure the button of my equally white dress suit was still buttoned. Then, one foot in front of the other, I stepped onto the stage of the pageant I'd been waiting my whole life to win.

Before I knew it, the opening model sequence, talent competition, and commercial presentation were over. This year, I did a commercial for my dad's Sky Pop show with little tiny onstage indoor fireworks. It was really cool. And no costume was needed, so I didn't violate *Secret Keeper Girl Club* rule number six.

It was time for the ballroom gown competition. Since I was the second to last one to compete in commercial presentation, I wasn't dressed. Most of the other girls were. Laney was ready to go in her pink dress and couldn't take her eyes off herself in her big round backstage mirror. Most of the other girls were dressed, too, and looked really pretty. I was glad I wasn't a judge.

Everyone here deserves to win, I thought to myself.

I glanced toward my gorgeous dress, which still hung on the hook next to my lighted dressing table.

Mrs. Anderson, Abbey's mom, started sweeping my hair into the updo we'd agreed on in dress rehearsal. As she put the finishing touches on it, Riley walked out of the bathroom in her ballroom gown.

Everyone inhaled all at once when they saw her, and it wasn't because she looked beautiful, even though she did.

"What?" pleaded Riley, wondering what was wrong.

I knew right away she was in big trouble. And there was no time to fix it. Her slim, fitted dress was black with big white polka dots and a pretty red belt. It was sleeveless, too. The pageant rules ran through my head.

"Riley, you idiot!" shrieked Laney. "Didn't you read the pageant rules? Your dress has to be all one color! *And* it has to have a puffy skirt. *And* it has to have sleeves!"

The color drained from Riley's face and she looked like she might burst into tears. Mrs. Butter's words ran through my head, "Be sure to go over your rules carefully." I knew that the second she stepped out onto that stage, she was going to be disqualified.

"How could you do this?" Laney whined. She stomped around again. This time it looked like maybe someone had stolen her entire collection of Barbies.

No one seemed to know what to do. Not even Mrs. Anderson, who was the only adult backstage. I could hear the music starting for the ballroom gown contest, and they called "Abbey Anderson." Abbey rushed to get composed and headed out to the stage. Her mom was distracted by peering through the curtain to watch.

Riley only had about ten minutes and then she was finished!

"What do I do?" Riley asked, looking at me. Suddenly Mrs. Hefty's wonderful face came to my mind and I knew *exactly* what to do.

"Come here," I ordered. And I started working the plan in my head.

I checked my look in the mirror.

No time for banana berry lip gloss, I thought. I decided my lips could go au naturel!

"Danika McAllister!" I heard my name called from in front of the curtain.

When I stepped out onstage, the lights hit me in the

eyes, which made it easy to avoid the gaze of the judges.
Instead, I looked at my fan club. At first Mom looked
completely shocked and confused, then she looked super
sad. Mrs. Hefty and Mrs. V, knowing the rules well, looked
at each other with concern. Everyone else was clueless and
had insanely huge smiles smeared across their faces.

"Go, Danika!" the Secret Keeper Girls yelled in unison.
Little did they know.

When I arrived at my appointed place on the stage,
I posed and waited for Riley to make her grand entrance.

"Riley Peterson!" said the MC.

The dramatic orchestra music crescendoed as if on
cue, and the spotlight found the center of the curtain.
Invisible drawstrings pulled the curtain back until the
audience could see just the bottom of a full skirt in the
shadows.

One dainty, white satin ballerina slipper raised the
front of the skirt and made its way into the spotlight.

Then the dress seemed to glide into view.

Riley Peterson emerged in my one-of-a-kind dress.
Mrs. Anderson had whipped her hair up into a bun and
even managed to add a few tiny pin curls here and there.
Riley's chestnut brown hair with natural summer high-

lights went great with my dress. The sequins caught the lights, and the dress shimmered as she walked. The crowd seemed to stop breathing for a moment, and I looked over at Mom. She was beaming with pride and wiping tears from her eyes.

I guess she liked my black-and-white polka-dotted dress with the red belt.

I couldn't help myself.

I started to cry, too.

I knew I'd just won something, but it wasn't the Miss Teeny Pop crown, that's for sure.

Fifteen minutes after the new Miss Teeny Pop, Abbey Anderson, was crowned, I came out from back-stage wearing grey sweats and a pink T-shirt with my ballerina flats. Mom and Dad were there waiting with all my most favorite people in the whole world. I could tell by the looks on their faces that Mom had filled them in on the whole dress thing.

Before I knew it, I had practically an entire flower shop of flowers in my arms and everyone was hugging me.

Nai Nai pulled me aside between hugs and photos and said, "We go home. Make egg drop soup."

"Actually, Nai Nai, I don't really think I need any!" I said.

She beamed with pride.

"Before you leave, can you come out to my car with Kate, Toni, and Yuzi?" asked Mrs. V. "There's something Mrs. Hefty wants to give you."

What could it be?

Danika's Totally Terrible Tess

CHAPTER 10

Show Stopper

OK, new best-day-**ever.** This was it.

I walked through the red doors of the Rutherford B. Hayes cafeteria. I wasn't alone. Kate, Toni, and Yuzi were with me. We'd stayed up late last night IMing a plan for reentry into the crazy world of the Rutherford B. Hayes middle school cafeteria.

I winked at Mrs. Hefty when she saw us coming. She smiled real big, then waddled off to do her job.

Everyone was there.

The brainiacs had their lunches pushed to the side so they could play chess.

The jocks were laughing at Trevor Kenworth, who was making burping sounds with his armpit.

The planet savers were all sitting together with their backs to their table. They had duct tape on their mouths and signs about global warming taped to their chests.

The popular girls were at their regular table in the middle of the room. They were all wearing pink in tribute to Laney, who came in second runner-up last night. She was obviously telling them all about it.

"And then I realized that my girl Riley was in so much trouble," she said. Laney made a fake sad face. Riley looked like she'd finally had enough.

Me, Kate, Toni, and Yuzi just plopped ourselves down at the table. We hadn't been invited. In fact, no one had even voted us in, but we made ourselves right at home and began opening our lunches.

"Eww! Baloney again," said Yuzi. "My mom is having a bad lunch week. Trade, anyone?"

"I'll trade," said Toni. "I love baloney. Want my turkey and tomato?"

We acted like nothing unusual had just happened, but something very unusual was happening. The unwritten rules of lunchroom power had just been challenged. Laney was standing up now.

"What do you think you are doing?" she asked, glaring at me.

"Oh, this?" I said, taking a bite of my tuna salad sand-wich. "This is called eating."

Everyone laughed except her little cotton candy fan club. Their eyes were wide.

"This is *our* table," said Laney. She made an annoying little circle with her two pointy fingers as she pointed to the table.

"Oh, you can sit here," said Kate. "It's just fine with us."

"Yep," I said. "It's fine with us."

Then we went back to our eating.

Laney looked like she was about to throw a temper tantrum the size of Jupiter. She flittered up and down on her tiptoes and her cheeks turned bright red. Her mouth was wide open as if she were about to scream, but nothing came out. Just when I thought she might burst, she flopped herself back down into her seat and just fumed in silence.

I smiled thinking of the club rules we wrote last night while we were IMing.

RULE #8: Always sit together at lunch.

RULE #9: Anyone who wants to can totally hang with us at lunch.

RULE #10: There will be no voting on who can be whose friend!

"Riley, I'm glad you won the ballroom gown competition," I said, looking right at her. "You looked majorly beautiful in my dress!"

"Thanks," she said, and looked down shyly at her food.

"Ewwww!" wailed Laney, finally erupting into the full screech she'd been holding inside. "You *cannot* sit here!"

"Sure we can. And you can, too!" I said calmly, looking right into her eyes. Then I spoke a little more loudly, "Anyone who wants to can sit with us!"

"Cool," said Ferner, coming out of nowhere and plopping down next to us.

"Ferner," whined Laney, "what are you *doing*?"

"Just sitting with my second grade do-si-do partner, Laney," he said, staring her down. "Got a problem with that?" Suddenly, I decided that I actually did like him.

Laney looked at him like she didn't understand the language he'd just spoken.

There was an awkward silence followed by a dragging sound. Riley Peterson slid her cafeteria tray closer to me and smiled shyly.

I'm thinking that with a little time, she just might make a great Secret Keeper Girl.

I took another bite of my tuna and looked over at Mrs. Hefty. She gave me a thumbs-up.

Yep, this is definitely my new best-day-ever. And the best part hasn't even happened yet!

Spotlights raced through the Spectra Dome and shone on Alayna Rayne as she belted out her number one hit song twenty feet from me.

"I've gotta slow down, wa-a-ay down.
This earth is spinnin' round and round,
Don't wanna miss this moment's sound
Gotta be who I am now;
Who I am right now!"

As the song came to an end, fireworks went off onstage behind her. My dad told me earlier that he had helped her manager set that up. I had bragged about that on the way here.

"This is the best," Kate screamed at me even though her mouth was practically inside my ear cavity. "I'm so blown away!"

The surprise that Mrs. Hefty had for us after the Teeny Pop Pageant was six—not four—but *six* front-row seats to the Alayna Rayne concert. Mrs. Hefty and Mrs. V had been on the committee to collect prizes for this year's pageant winners. It turned out that they were the ones who'd gotten the tickets to the concert to begin with. Always looking for their own brand of fun, they had talked their husbands and the Butters into using the extra six tickets. But when they saw what happened at the pageant, they decided that the new Secret Keeper Girls should get them instead. (They kept two though, so they could come with us!)

"I love you, Ohio!" hollered Alayna as her song came to an end. "Tonight we have a special guest in the house." I knew she was going to introduce Abbey Anderson, who was seated right next to me with her parents, and was wearing her crown. Mrs. Hefty had told us that Abbey was going to get to go onstage with Alayna as a part of her prize.

"I'd like to introduce Abbey Anderson, who is Marion, Ohio's, newest Miss Teeny Pop!" said Alayna. The spotlight searched the front row looking for Abbey, who was already standing and waving. Finally, it found her.

"I met Abbey backstage before the concert," said Alayna. "She said she has someone she wants to dedicate this next song to—someone who taught her about being a true friend. In fact, Abbey and the very first Miss Teeny Pop have something special to present."

Suddenly Abbey and Mrs. Hefty were escorted by two of Alayna's bodyguards to the big set of stairs in the middle of the stage. Two more bodyguards grabbed my arms and practically lifted me off the ground as they followed the first two.

What in the world? I wondered.

"Abbey. Mrs. Hefty," said Alayna as they reached her onstage. She handed Mrs. Hefty her mic.

Abbey just smiled, and I realized then that her hands were behind her back. What was she holding?

"Well, there," began Mrs. Hefty in rapid pace. She went on to tell the audience the whole crazy story, starting with the Purple Flurp, which made everyone laugh, and ending with Riley Peterson in my one-of-a-kind dress, which made everyone cry.

"There's a saying that if you want to have a friend, you have to be one. In the spirit of the Miss Teeny Pop Pageant, we want to present this, the first Miss Teeny Pop crown . . . "

She paused and Abbey pulled out that old, slightly bent plastic crown that I'd seen at Mrs. Hefty's house just two days ago. It looked beautiful tonight.

". . . to someone who is definitely a true friend . . . Miss Danika McAllister!"

Abbey walked over to me, carefully pulled my sky-blue headband from my head, and placed the *original* Miss Teeny Pop crown on *me!*

I was wearing the Miss Teeny Pop crown!

"You're the true winner," Abbey whispered to me. Then she hugged me.

104

"This song is dedicated to Danika McAllister!" shouted Alayna, and she started singing "Tru Friends R Tru."

I can't lie. It was pretty sweet standing there under a dozen spotlights and wearing the Miss Teeny Pop crown as Alayna Rayne sang to me. I loved it, even if it took me a whole lot longer than expected to get here. I'm actually glad it did. I needed to take a few "walks," as Mrs. V called them, and it was worth every step to find true friends along the way.

I was pretty sure that I'd probably eventually put my new crown in a trunk somewhere. I might even totally get over my obsession with the Miss Teeny Pop Pageant one day.

But I'd **never** outgrow my true friends.

Tru Friends R Tru

☆ Danika, Kate, Toni, and Yuzi's ☆

Secret Keeper Girl Club Rules

🌀 RULE #1: Always keep each other's secrets!

✻ RULE #2: No boys allowed! ☆

🌀 RULE #3: Only wear banana berry flavored lip gloss.

✻ RULE #4: Eat a lot of egg drop soup.

SKG forever!

🌀 RULE #5: Wise friends stand beside each other through tough times. Foolish ones just come to the parties. Be there!

✻ RULE #6: No costumes ever . . . especially produce. ☆

🌀 RULE #7: Be a friend. It's the only way to have one!

✻ RULE #8 Always sit together at lunch.

🌀 RULE #9 Anyone who wants to can totally hang with us at lunch.

✻ Rule #10 There will be no voting on who can be whose friend. 🌀🌀

Girl Gab About True Friendship

Hey, Secret Keeper Girl! Grab your mom or a BFF for some great girl gab about true friendship. Let's take a look at what you can learn from Danika's crazy quest for the Teeny Pop crown. First, she learned that she wasn't such a great friend, but then she learned how to be one!

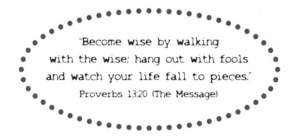

"Become wise by walking with the wise; hang out with fools and watch your life fall to pieces."
Proverbs 13:20 (The Message)

Gab About It:

Hopefully, you could see this Bible verse literally lived out in Danika's life. As she hung around with "fools" like Riley, her life fell to pieces. As she began to hang out with friends who wanted what was best for her, like Kate, she made better choices.

💜 What do you think it means to be wise? ....

....

....

....

💜 How do we "walk" with someone who is wise?.....................

....

....

....

💜 What bad decisions did Danika make when she hung out
with Laney? (Hint: There were two big ones!)

....

....

....

💜 What did Mrs. Hefty say was the most important thing
about friendship? (Hint: It became SKG Rule #7)

....

....

....

💙 Have you ever had a friend like Laney, who seemed to lead you into bad decisions? ....

....

....

....

💙 Is there someone like Kate (who didn't really have a friend at the beginning of the book) or Riley (who needed a better friend) in your life? Who do you think God might want you to be friends with? ....

....

....

....

PRAY IT OUT LOUD! Danika learned how to *be* a friend! It's so easy to get stressed about who likes you and who thinks you're cool. Instead, we should be thinking about who needs a good friend to walk with her. Ask God to show you a wise friend who needs someone to walk with. Pray it out loud with your mom!

Danika's Totally Terrible Toss

MORE

SeCret Keeper GIRL
FICTION SERIES

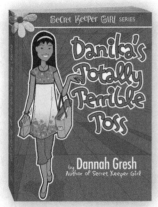

ISBN-13: 978-0-8024-8702-5

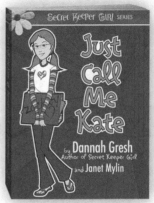

ISBN-13: 978-0-8024-8703-2

ISBN-13: 978-0-8024-8704-9

ISBN-13: 978-0-8024-8705-6

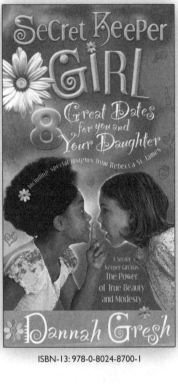